W9-CYA-182

© 1995, Landoll, Inc.
Ashland, Ohio 44805
® The Landoll Apple Logo is a trademark owned by Landoll, Inc.
and is registered with the U. S. Patent and Trademark Office.
No part of this book may be reproduced or copied.
All rights reserved. Manufactured in the U.S.A.

PAUL BUNYAN

STORYBOOK

A long time ago, when the trees were taller than they are today and their trunks were so thick that it took an ordinary man an hour just to walk around them, men in the timber camps throughout America liked to tell stories about a woodsman so big and so strong that the ground shook beneath his feet as he walked through the forest. He was so tall that the biggest trees barely reached to his belt. His name was Paul Bunyan.

Paul wore a knit hat on top his head, and his glossy black hair and beard were impressive beneath it. His eyebrows, which covered a fourth of his forehead, were also black and his mustache had natural curls.

He had bright yellow long johns and his bulky, flannel shirt boasted huge red and white checks. Bright wool socks showed above his black boots which had buckskin laces and big brass eyelets and hooks.

Paul lived in a huge cave beside a lake in the far north. His home was filled with books, for he was a student who wished to learn about all things.

One day, while Paul was studying in his favorite chair, there came a mighty blizzard — the beginning of the great blue snow. Animals fled from this snow that was so deep and so different in color.

The moose herds – which in those days were so thick that Paul had to chase them off because their loud chewing interfered with his studies – ran so far that only a few of them are around in the woods today. And when Paul's mighty moose hound, Niagara, realized that the snow which was falling on him was blue instead of white like it had always been, why, he was so surprised that he ran off too!

Niagara's long legs carried him so fast that he soon passed the bears that were running because the elk did; and then passed the elk that were running because they thought the bears were chasing them.

He might have gone on forever, but just as he gained full speed, he ran into the North Pole and knocked down ninety feet of ice. Niagara felt so foolish that he never came home again.

Meanwhile, snug in his cave, Paul Bunyan was not aware of all the terrible things that were happening outside. It was not until he heard a loud crashing sound and broke through the blue snow drifts outside his cave that he found the ice, which had formed seven feet thick over the bay, was now breaking up.

Far out in the water, Paul could see something strange breaking through the ice. As it came closer, he could make out two ears – each the size of a barn door. And when Paul waded out a mile or so through the ice, he found a baby ox. It was blue, like the snow which was falling, and many times bigger than an ordinary animal of its sort.

Paul figured the baby ox must have become lost from its mother during the blizzard. So he followed a trail of smashed trees and crumpled boulders from where his new friend had fallen and rolled into the water. But there was no sign of the baby ox's parents.

He carried the shivering animal to his cave and propped it in front of the fireplace wrapped in blankets. Paul named him Babe, because the ox reminded him of a baby all wrapped in swaddling clothes. He could find nothing else a baby ox might like to eat, so he fed it moose moss – which Babe seemed to love.

Babe grew bigger and stronger every day, but still stayed blue. Soon he was butting Paul all around the cave, and Paul realized he must find a way to make use of Babe's mighty energy.

Paul had a brilliant idea...huge trees grew all across America. He would make them into logs, and the logs would become boards for houses and furniture for everyone who wanted to live in this great country.

There were no tools in those days, so at first Paul just uprooted trees as he walked through the forest. To get them to market, he tied two-ton bundles on each side of Babe. As the ox grew older, he was able to carry more and more.

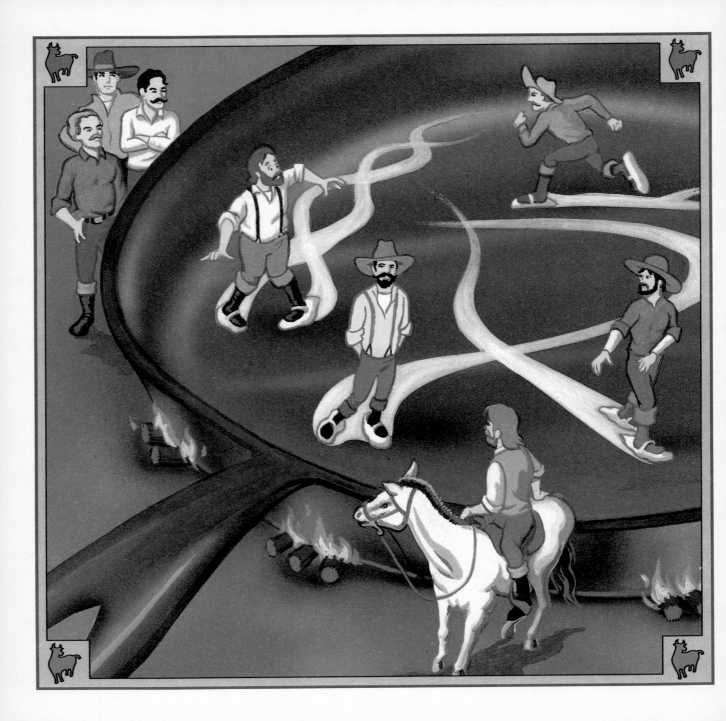

When men from all over heard about this new business Paul Bunyan was in, they flocked to his campsite to work with him. Paul had to concoct saws, axes, and other tools for the workers who couldn't uproot trees and break them in half with their hands as he did.

Paul's new business grew rapidly. He needed cooks to feed him and his hungry crew. The kitchen covered acres with great ovens to bake pies, cakes and puddings; bins for potatoes and other vegetables; fruit and vinegar cellars; sugar barrels; sauerkraut tanks, a frankfurter shed; and an air-tight onion room.

There was a griddle so large that three dozen cooks could stand around its edge flipping pancakes. Four more men would wrap towels soaked in lard around their feet and skate inside the griddle to grease it.

Between meals, Paul's army of loggers cut trees at such a great rate that they must walk farther and farther to work each day. Soon it was taking longer to reach the trees than it did to cut them.

It was time for Paul to come up with a practical solution. He made a sled to haul the men to work. It had to be big enough to carry several hundred men. But what could pull it? Then he remembered Babe, the great blue ox, who grew stronger every day on a diet of moose moss, and left-over pies and doughnuts from the kitchen.

Babe now measured 42 axe handles between his horns. An ordinary man standing at his front end had to use a telescope to see his hind legs. He ran so fast that only Paul Bunyan could keep up with the sled to guide Babe, and many of the loggers became seasick every morning during the wild ride.

There must be another way to solve the problem. Luckily, Paul Bunyan, besides being taller than any tree and stronger than one hundred men put together, was also very smart.

Early one morning, he gathered ten miles of heavy chain, took Babe and ran thirty miles to the nearest forest. Circling enough trees to make a day's work for his men, Paul bundled his chain around them and hooked it to Babe, who by then could pull anything.

When Paul's crew came out of the kitchen after breakfast that morning, they were astounded to find that there would be no long, wild ride to work. Bunyan had pulled the woods to them!

After Paul cut down all the trees in sight, and built dozens of cities and a few smaller towns, he and Babe paddled out to sea on a great raft, throwing clods of dirt over the side from time to time to create islands and grow new trees. And that's the last that was seen of Paul Bunyan and Babe, the mighty blue ox.